Great Jobs in the Skilled Trades

W.L. Kitts

San Diego, CA

About the Author
W.L. Kitts is a professional freelance writer and children's book author who lives in San Diego, California.

© 2019 ReferencePoint Press, Inc.
Printed in the United States

For more information, contact:
ReferencePoint Press, Inc.
PO Box 27779
San Diego, CA 92198
www.ReferencePointPress.com

ALL RIGHTS RESERVED.
No part of this work covered by the copyright hereon may be reproduced or used in any form or by any means—graphic, electronic, or mechanical, including photocopying, recording, taping, web distribution, or information storage retrieval systems—without the written permission of the publisher.

Picture Credits:

Cover: zstockphotos/iStockphoto.com
 6: Maury Aaseng
11: kurhan/Shutterstock.com
28: shinobi/Shutterstock.com
43: sirtravelalot/Shutterstock.com
58: Kzenon/Shutterstock.com
66: Basyn/Shutterstock.com

LIBRARY OF CONGRESS CATALOGING-IN-PUBLICATION DATA

Name: Kitts, W.L., author.
Title: Great Jobs in the Skilled Trades/by W.L. Kitts.
Description: San Diego, CA: ReferencePoint Press, [2018] | Series: Great Jobs | Audience: Grade 9 to 12. | Includes bibliographical references and index.
Identifiers: LCCN 2018031419 (print) | LCCN 2018033047 (ebook) | ISBN 9781682825266 (eBook) | ISBN 9781682825259 (hardback)
Subjects: LCSH: Skilled labor—Juvenile literature.
Classification: LCC HD3629 (ebook) | LCC HD3629 .K538 2018 (print) | DDC 331.7/94—dc23
LC record available at https://lccn.loc.gov/2018031419

Contents

Introduction: Hands-On Careers	4
Plumber	9
Electrician	17
Welder	25
Automotive Technician	33
Solar Photovoltaic Installer	41
Wind Turbine Technician	49
Chef	57
Hairstylist	65
Interview with a Hairstylist	73
Other Jobs in the Skilled Trades	76
Index	77

Introduction
Hands-On Careers

What do plumbers, landscapers, and chefs have in common? They fall under the wide-ranging occupational category of skilled trades. People looking to work in the trades often complete one- to two-year programs that teach essential skills in addition to on-the-job training. The work itself often requires hands-on labor and can be physically demanding. Tradespeople generally like working with their hands and feeling the satisfaction of a job well done.

In an interview with the Career Foundation, a Canadian online employment service, an arborist encourages those who enjoy working with their hands to consider this career. She says, "Working in the trades, there is never any question at the end of the day as to what you've accomplished. Your achievement is right in front of you, whether it be a tree pruned, a section framed, or a pipe laid."

Though the majority of tradespeople work in the construction or manufacturing industries, workers in this field may also be found in a variety of industries, including food service, cosmetology, and automotive. Some may have opportunities in more than one. A welder, for example, could find employment in construction, manufacturing, and the energy industry, among others. And all tradespeople have the opportunity to be self-employed.

Earn While You Learn

A high school diploma is the minimum educational requirement for most jobs in the skilled trades. However, many applicants need further education and training, which they can obtain through technical institutes, trade schools, and community colleges. Programs can last anywhere from six weeks for truck driving, for example, to two years for plumbing. This means a tradesperson can enter the workforce faster than many other occupations.

Many who want to become a tradesperson apply for paid apprenticeships. Apprentices take course work as well as complete a specific number of hours of hands-on training under an experienced tradesperson. The opportunity to earn while one learns is a big advantage. A person will not be mired in debt upon leaving school and trying to find a job. Plus, an apprentice will already have a job, since most apprenticeships are paid for by the apprentice's employer. And although apprentices typically earn 30 percent to 50 percent less than their experienced counterparts, these jobs tend to be well paid.

Many trades require credentials or licenses to work. Credentials vary by state and locality, and some employers (and unions) will pay for them. Most tradespeople continually upgrade their skills and education, especially around safety. Achieving specialized skills and certifications are how most tradespeople advance. More skills equal more opportunities and higher salaries.

Although parts of these jobs could be automated, like the use of robotics in welding, it is highly unlikely that many jobs in the skilled trades will be outsourced. A toilet cannot be fixed from outside the country. Hands-on jobs require people on-site locally.

Solid Future and Growth

At present, there are more skilled trades jobs than people to fill them, particularly in the concrete, electrical, and drywall trades. United States Gypsum, a building products manufacturing company, and the US Chamber of Commerce publish a quarterly account on the state of the construction industry called the *Commercial Construction Index*. According to the index, contractors are concerned about labor shortages, particularly in commercial construction, a trend that started in early 2017.

The thriving construction industry is not the only reason for the shortage. There has been a trend of educators encouraging students to reject vocational and trade schools in favor of universities. Plus, the trades have been dominated by baby boomers,

Great Jobs in Skilled Trades

Occupation	Minimum Educational Requirements	2017 Median Pay
Boilermaker	Apprenticeship program	$62,260
Construction laborer and helper	On-the-job training	$33,450
Drywall and ceiling installer, and taper	On-the-job training	$43,970
Drafter	Associate's degree	$54,170
Barber, hairstylist, cosmetologist	State-approved program and license	$24,900
Industrial machinery mechanic, machinery maintanence worker, millwright	High school diploma or equivalent	$50,440
Ironworker	High school diploma or equivalent	$51,320
Machinist	On-the-job training	$44,110
Pest control worker	High school diploma or equivalent	$34,370
Plumber, pipefitter, steamfitter	High school diploma or equivalent	$52,590
Heavy and tractor-trailer truck driver	High school diploma and professional truck driving school	$42,480
Welder, cutter, solderer, brazer	High school diploma or equivalent	$40,240

Source: Bureau of Labor Statistics, *Occupational Outlook Handbook*, 2018. www.bls.gov.

many of whom have reached retirement age. Add to these factors the growth of new industries like wind and solar energy and it is easy to see why there are shortages.

Even the US government is attempting to mitigate the problem. In 2017 President Donald Trump issued an executive order calling for the promotion and expansion of apprenticeship programs. One of the goals of the executive order is to make it easier for young people to enter a career in the skilled trades.

Opportunities for skilled tradespeople are expected to continue. The American Welding Society predicts that by 2024 there will be four hundred thousand unfilled welding jobs. The increased demand is good for anyone considering working in this field. Higher demand equals increased wages.

Women and the Skilled Trades

One way to solve the job shortage crisis is to recruit women. Many trades jobs are traditionally male-dominated. And unions in particular, like the United Association—Union of Plumbers, Fitters, Welders and Service Techs, are reaching out to women to help fill shortages and create a more diverse workforce.

Most skilled trades offer women greater income potential than jobs in female-dominated fields like child care or administrative assistants. According to the Bureau of Labor Statistics, the median salaries for these two occupations in 2017 were $22,290 and $37,870 respectively. By contrast, the median salary for an electrician was $54,110.

However, because of gender stereotypes (by both men and women), women considering a career in skilled trades are often concerned about working in male-dominated fields. The website Electrician Careers Guide explored this subject in a survey of female electricians. According to the results of the survey, listed in the article "Is It Difficult to Be a Female Electrician?," most women had positive work experiences:

> There were some old-timers who gave them a hard time, but one woman reported that most of the older guys

just treated them like daughters. One woman even noted that she had worked in the corporate world . . . and the treatment she got from the executive types was much worse. . . . Other women have said that whatever sexism they faced was similar to the sexism they faced as waiters, office workers, etc.

Overall, the women surveyed found that if they did their jobs, most of their male counterparts treated them the same as men.

Rewarding, Tangible Work

The skilled trades are not for everyone. But for those who like to work with their hands and want or need to get started on a decent-paying career in a relatively short period of time, learning a skilled trade may be a good choice. And best of all, people who work in the skilled trades enjoy the satisfaction of seeing a job well done at the end of the day.

Plumber

What Does a Plumber Do?

Plumbers see a lot of clogged sinks and plugged toilets. But they do much more than opening up blockages in household bathrooms and kitchens. Plumbers are responsible for the systems that enable liquids and gases to travel from one place to another. They install, maintain, and repair pipes that carry water, sewage, and gas to and from residential, commercial, and industrial properties. They also work on septic fields, waste-holding tanks not connected to a sewage system.

Plumbers often work with other tradespeople in the construction industry to design plumbing systems for new or renovated structures. Working directly with contractors, plumbers determine specifications for water, waste, and venting systems. This process requires knowledge of building codes and other systems, like wiring. Plumbers also prepare budgets and materials lists before doing the physical work of measuring, cutting, bending, threading, soldering, and laying pipes.

Many plumbers are self-employed and may be responsible

At a Glance

Plumber

Minimum Educational Requirements
High school diploma or equivalency

Personal Qualities
People skills, problem-solving abilities, physical strength, manual dexterity

Certification and Licensing
License after two to five years as an apprentice

Working Conditions
Indoors/outdoors, possible extreme temperatures and foul-smelling situations

Salary Range
About $27,000 to $100,000 or more

Number of Jobs
Close to 500,000 as of 2016*

Future Job Outlook
Growth of 16 percent through 2026

* Includes plumbers, pipefitters, and steamfitters

for running a business as well. And all plumbers are lifelong learners. Plumbers are expected to be up-to-date on their industry, as well as on safety standards and building regulations.

Whether self-employed or working for someone else, plumbers earn good money. Dave Jones, a regional vice president with Roto-Rooter Plumbers, came from a long line of police officers. But he took a different path. Jones started trade school while still in high school, and after his first full year as a plumber, he was making more money than his father. In an online promotional video for Roto-Rooter, Jones says, "I've talked to friends . . . who have come out of college . . . we have a lot of plumbers on staff that make more money than what they make. You can make a very good living being a plumber. I have no regrets . . . at all."

How Do You Become a Plumber?

Education

Becoming a plumber is a blend of practical, hands-on experience and study. Each state has its own licensing requirements. In most states, however, a licensed plumber must be at least eighteen years old and have a high school diploma or equivalency. High school students who are interested in this career will want to take courses in shop, algebra, geometry, and (if available) thermodynamics.

One route to a plumbing career is through a community college, trade school, or online institute. Students can earn a one- or two-year certification or associate's degree in plumbing. Costs vary, depending on factors like state of residency and whether there is a need for room and board.

Apprenticeships and Licensing

The most common way to get a job as a plumber is to become a plumber's apprentice (or plumber's helper), working under the guidance of a licensed master plumber. Apprenticeships are often offered through unions, industry associations, businesses, and even the US Army. Apprentices are paid to work full-time while taking required course work in their off hours.

Repairing clogged sinks and toilets are not the only jobs plumbers do. They also install, maintain, and repair pipes that carry water, sewage, and gas to and from residential, commercial, and industrial buildings.

Course work focuses on practical skills and subject areas. Soldering, cutting and laying pipes, blueprint reading, and drafting are among the practical skills that an apprentice learns. They also study subjects like physics and applied chemistry along with building codes and safety training.

Apprentices usually receive approximately 250 hours of class time along with 2,000 hours of on-the-job training, which usually takes about four or five years. Once the requirements of the apprenticeship are satisfied, apprentices may apply to take the plumber's license exam in their state. If successful, they will advance to the second level on the road to becoming a plumber—a journey worker.

Journey workers are still required to work under a licensed master plumber, but they have more independence than they did as an apprentice. They also bring home larger paychecks. After two more years of on-the-job training, a journey worker may apply to be a master plumber, the third and final level.

Depending on state requirements, this stage will require even more courses in advance of taking the master plumber exam.

If they pass the exam, they will receive their master plumber license, which means they can finally work on their own and earn an even larger salary.

Skills and Personality

Plumbers work with a wide range of people—individuals, contractors, and others in the skilled trades—so people skills are key to being successful in this career. Construction managers can be challenging during long hours and tight deadlines, and private clients can be short on patience when they are faced with water or toilet issues. So plumbers need to have good listening and communication skills to deal with everyone in a professional manner.

Plumbers need a variety of other skills as well. Problem-solving skills are crucial as well as strong math skills, which help in developing a project budget or figuring out pipe angles or water volume. Good reading and comprehension ability are necessary, too, since plumbers need to read technical manuals and directions. And because a plumber has to work with multiple tools (often in small spaces), manual dexterity and mechanical abilities are vital. Among the tools in the plumber's toolbox are various wrenches to tighten or loosen bolts. Plumbers also use plungers and plumber's "snakes" to remove obstructions in blocked pipes. And when plumbers are laying or installing pipes, they might join them with a blowtorch, cut them with a hacksaw, or sand them down with a metal file.

Plumbing is a physically demanding job. It helps if a person considering this career is fit and strong. It is not unheard of for a plumber to hang upside down to access a pipe. This adds to the danger associated with the job. The Bureau of Labor Statistics' (BLS) *Occupational Outlook Handbook* states that plumbers "have one of the highest rates of injuries and illnesses of all occupations." On-the-job injuries include burns from blowtorches, cuts from pipe cutting, and falls from ladders.

According to Patrick Kellett, one of the most important qualities for a plumber is a good attitude. Kellett works for the United Association of Journeymen and Apprentices of the Plumbing and Pipe Fitting Industry of the United States, Canada. On the *U.S.*

News & World Report website, he says, "A positive attitude is also really important for a candidate's success . . . because this can be a kind of tough business and a dangerous business."

On the Job

Employers

According to the BLS, there were close to five hundred thousand plumbers, pipefitters, and steamfitters in 2016. Plumbers are often grouped in the same occupational category as pipefitters and steamfitters. (Pipefitters deal with pipes that carry chemicals, acids, and steam used in factories and power plants; steamfitters work with high-pressure liquids and gases). More than 72 percent of these tradespeople worked in the construction industry, with close to 13 percent identifying as self-employed.

Plumbers usually specialize in residential new construction, commercial new construction, or service and repair of existing plumbing (both residential and commercial). For those who work in construction, their jobs are subject to the rise and fall of the economy. However, plumbers who work in service and repair will have a more stable career.

Working Conditions

Plumbers tend to work long hours. When dealing with emergencies (and a backed-up sewer or a plugged toilet can be a real emergency), the standard forty-hour workweek can easily turn into eighty hours.

Even when not dealing with emergencies, plumbing work can be challenging. In a video on the ePlumbingCourses website, a residential plumber named Luke explains that a plumber might be working in a small, cramped space like an attic with no air-conditioning one day, digging a ditch outside in 100°F (38°C) weather the next, or fixing a broken pipe in freezing temperatures another. Luke admits conditions can also get "pretty nasty" and extremely smelly when working on sewage pipes or in a septic field. "People say it stinks, but to me I got to make a joke out of it and I say, 'it smells like money.'" Luke is quick to add, "It's a lot of hard work, but it pays off."

According to 2016 BLS data, 98.6 percent of plumbers are men. However, this is starting to change. Laurie Bence began her career as a plumber in the Army National Guard. She is licensed as a master plumber in Massachusetts and a journey worker in Rhode Island. In a 2016 interview in the online magazine *Plumbing & Mechanical*, Bence says, "Being a woman in a male-dominated trade has challenged me but also inspired me to prove to myself and others that I can do it and be good at it. If you work hard and acquire the knowledge needed to get the job done, it will pay off as it has for me."

Bence urges other young women to consider a career in plumbing. "If you don't mind getting your hands dirty, then take a leap. It is a very rewarding field financially, physically and mentally."

Earnings

Plumbers enjoy stable employment. According to *U.S. News & World Report*'s "Best Jobs Rankings" for 2018, a plumber is the number one best construction job when it comes to factors like pay, stress level, job market, and future. Wages range from about $27,000 to $100,000 or even more for a master plumber. Apprentices generally make 30 percent to 50 percent less than journey workers and master plumbers.

Opportunities for Advancement

Many master plumbers open their own businesses. The financial rewards of running a business can be great, but the added time and energy required can be challenging. Not everyone wants to be a business owner, however. For these plumbers, advancement usually follows the stages of apprentice to journey worker to master plumber, which can take anywhere from six to eight years.

What Is the Future Outlook for Plumbers?

The future job outlook is pretty solid for plumbers. Generally, growth in construction-related jobs is directly proportional to the economy. When the economy is booming, so is the construction sector, and vice versa. That being said, plumbers are always in demand, regardless of what is going on with the rest of the industry.

Currently, there is a push for both new and existing buildings to meet new water-efficiency standards. This is good news for plumbers and will translate into a higher demand for plumbers than usual. Also, with fewer young people taking up plumbing as a trade and older plumbers retiring in record numbers since the 2007–2009 recession, the industry is now facing a shortage of workers. All of this is in line with what the BLS forecasts—a 16 percent increase in jobs through 2026. This translates into roughly seventy-six thousand new jobs—faster than the average growth rate for all other jobs.

Plumbing services will always be needed. "It's not something you can outsource or ship overseas," Dave Jones explains. "Once you have this trade, you will never starve. You will never not be able to find a job."

Find Out More

ePlumbingCourses
website: www.eplumbingcourses.com

The ePlumbingCourses website is a plumbing resource that provides information on plumbing courses, schools, and state license requirements.

Plumbing Contractors of America (PCA)
1385 Piccard Dr.
Rockville, MD 20850
website: www.mcaa.org/pca

The PCA is the national representative that lobbies on behalf of the United Association of Journeymen and Apprentices of the Plumbing and Pipe Fitting Industry of the United States, Canada. The PCA features a wide range of plumbing webinars, podcasts, videos, and industry bulletins on its website.

Plumbing-Heating-Cooling Contractors Association (PHCC)
180 S. Washington St., Suite 100
Falls Church, VA 22046
website: www.phccweb.org

Founded in 1883, the PHCC is the oldest trade association for the plumbing, heating, and cooling industry. The PHCC website includes industry publications, training, technical support, and networking opportunities. The site also offers career resources for high school and postsecondary students, such as scholarship information, apprentice training, and career information.

PlumbingWEB.com
website: http://plumbingweb.com

PlumbingWEB.com is an online one-stop shop for all things plumbing. This website provides a comprehensive list of plumbing organizations, books, websites, and magazines.

United Association of Journeymen and Apprentices of the Plumbing and Pipe Fitting Industry of the United States, Canada (UA)
3 Park Place
Annapolis, MD 21401
website: www.ua.org

The UA represents close to 350,000 plumbers and plumbing-related technicians across North America. The UA website offers information on various certification and apprenticeship programs, as well as state licensing.

Electrician

What Does an Electrician Do?

Electricity is essential to everyday life. And so are electricians. Without either there would be no lights or video games or blow dryers. Basically, electricians install, maintain, and repair wiring in the buildings that people live, work, and play in every day.

These tradespeople often specialize. Specialties include residential (homes); commercial (businesses, schools, and hospitals); industrial (factories or power plants); and low voltage (voice/data/video, fiber optics, and cable). Electricians can further specialize by being a construction electrician (designing and installing lighting systems) or a service or maintenance electrician (repairing or upgrading existing systems). According to Jono Adams from the ToughNickel website, the majority specialize in commercial, industrial, or maintenance work. In an article titled "Everything You Need to Know About Becoming an Electrician," Adams says, "Although all licensed electricians will be able to do residential installation and repair work, specializing is where the big money is."

At a Glance

Electrician

Minimum Educational Requirements
High school diploma or equivalency

Personal Qualities
Critical-thinking skills, problem-solving ability, detail oriented, manual dexterity, hand-eye coordination, math abilities, people skills

Certification and Licensing
Licensing required

Working Conditions
Indoors/outdoors, small spaces, varying weather/temperatures, going up and down ladders with heavy equipment

Salary Range
About $32,000 to $90,000

Number of Jobs
About 667,000 as of 2016

Future Job Outlook
Growth of 9 percent through 2026

A related but separate occupational category is lineman. Linemen install and repair power lines and transformers. They work on the distribution end of things, connecting electricity from the power source (like the utility company) to the end user. There are also opportunities for electricians in the growing solar- and wind-power industries. Many electricians are hired to install solar panels or do electrical work for wind turbines.

Being an electrician has prestige. Adams explains, "It is a very well-respected profession within the construction trade, and it's actually considered by many to be THE top job within the industry."

How Do You Become an Electrician?

Education

Students interested in a career as an electrician would be helped by taking classes in algebra, geometry, physics, chemistry, and mechanical drawing. And if the goal is to be self-employed, they should also consider taking business and accounting courses.

There are certain requirements for being an electrician. A person must be at least eighteen years old, have a high school diploma (or equivalency), and obtain an apprenticeship. There are no postsecondary educational requirements; however, if a student cannot find an apprenticeship, he or she might consider attending a community college or trade school first.

There are both one-year certificate and two-year associate's degree electrician programs. Courses might include electrical theory, power systems, wiring, drafting, electronics, and building codes. Courses taken may be applied toward an apprenticeship program. Plus, getting the education first can help in obtaining an apprenticeship (and passing the entrance exam), as well as make a person more attractive to an employer. "Keep in mind, you do not need to go to a trade school or electrician school to become an electrician," writes one industry expert on the Electrician Careers Guide website. "Some people choose to go to school; others do not, and still have satisfying careers as electricians. If you can find an apprenticeship right off the bat, that should be your first choice."

Apprenticeships and Licensing

There are many routes to obtaining an apprenticeship. A high school graduate may get an entry-level job as an electrician's helper. Helpers basically do grunt work, like digging ditches, for low pay. They cannot advance but will gain on-the-job experience and contacts, which could lead to an apprenticeship. Some students find apprenticeships by contacting electricians, contractors, and unions that sponsor programs.

According to Jerry Higgins, an electrician with twenty-five years' experience, the best way to get an apprenticeship is by talking to contractors in person. In "Things You Should Know Before Entering an Electrician Apprenticeship Program" on ToughNickel, Higgins writes, "Ask to talk to someone about employment possibilities as an apprentice electrician. These contractors . . . are ALWAYS looking for an intelligent and motivated person who will make them some money down the line."

Higgins suggests contacting people between eight and nine o'clock in the morning. "This is the sweet spot that comes after the early morning hustle-and-bustle but before the boss leaves for morning meetings. If you can confidently walk in and make a good impression, they will quickly see that you might be worth some time and effort in training you."

Apprenticeship applicants must pass an aptitude test to demonstrate reading comprehension and math skills. If they fail, the test may be retaken after six months. Websites are available that help applicants prepare for the test so they do not risk losing an apprenticeship opportunity.

Apprentices receive on-the-job training under the supervision of a licensed journey worker (the level after apprentice). Apprenticeships take from three to five years and include 144 hours of formal education and 2,000 hours of training, depending on the speciality and previous course work. An apprentice can expect to work full-time (and get paid for it) and take classes during off time.

Once the apprenticeship is completed, the apprentice advances to journey worker. Journey workers work without supervision; however, most states require licensing. Licensing requirements vary by state and often include a test to ensure journey workers are up-to-date on industry codes and safety standards.

Skills and Personality

Electricians need to be in good shape because the job can be physically demanding. Electricians often must jam themselves into small spaces, climb stairs and ladders with heavy tools, and stand or kneel for long periods.

Electricians need a variety of skills. Good reading comprehension is a must because electricians often receive their work orders in writing or via e-mail. Math skills are important as well, especially algebra, to determine things like the voltage or amps required. Among the tools electricians must learn to use are wire cutters, wire strippers, screwdrivers, power drills, saws, and specialized equipment like voltage meters. Electricians also need critical-thinking and problem-solving skills to diagnose and repair electrical issues. They need people skills too, since electricians often work with other tradespeople or deal with customers.

Electrical work is detailed. Electricians need manual dexterity and good eye-hand coordination for focused close-up work. And of primary importance is the ability to distinguish colors because wires are color coded. Safety is crucial in this trade. Part of an electrician's job is to ensure electrical work is up to code. Safety standards must be observed since they are literally a matter of life and death in this industry. If the wrong wires get crossed, it could result in fire or electrocution.

Being an electrician is considered one of the easier trades. Higgins explains, "Electricians don't need to work nearly as hard as many of the other tradesmen. For sure there is difficult work involved but electrical workers do a lot of thinking and planning before actually starting with the work."

Adams agrees. He writes, "You definitely won't have to push yourself to the limit physically to get the job done. The job is really about using your head as much as your hands, so if you're good at problem solving and have an eye for detail, this would definitely be the perfect job for you."

On the Job

Employers
Electricians held about 667,000 jobs in 2016, according to the Bureau of Labor Statistics (BLS). The majority of them worked for contractors (65 percent), with many fewer identifying as self-employed (8 percent).

In addition to being hired by contractors, electricians may also be hired by private electrical companies. Commercial and industrial electricians may work directly for schools, office buildings, retail stores, hospitals, manufacturing facilities, and power plants. Low-voltage electricians may work at any of the above settings as well as Internet and cable companies.

Working Conditions
Electricians generally work full-time. Those who work in construction or take emergency calls often work evenings and weekends as well as overtime. Service electricians primarily work regular hours. Self-employed electricians often have more control over their hours.

Because these tradespeople work both indoors and outdoors, they are at the mercy of the weather and varying temperatures. They might do wiring inside a crawl space with no air-conditioning on a sweltering day or work outside in the cold.

And according to the BLS, electricians have more injuries than most other trades. Electrical shocks, burns, and falls are common.

Earnings
U.S. News & World Report's "Best Jobs Rankings" for 2018 lists electrician as the number three best construction job. The rankings are based on factors like job stress, job prospects, and salary.

In 2016 the median wage for an electrician was $52,720, according to the BLS. The salary range for electricians was about

$32,000 to over $90,000. An apprentice usually earns about 30 percent to 50 percent less than trained electricians.

On the Electrician Careers Guide website, an article titled "Is Electrician a Good Career Choice?" states:

> Electricians earn a really, really good living. . . . The income that an electrician makes is higher than the average income of any other kind of worker, in *47 out of the 50 states*. That's pretty incredible. It's even more incredible when you consider that most electricians don't have as much student loan debt as those other people making more than the average state income. Note that we wrote, "Good Living" and not "Great Living." If you want to be filthy rich, go into banking. Or, actually, become a journeyman electrician and then start your own company!

Opportunities for Advancement

Electricians have opportunities for advancement throughout their careers. Service electricians may work their way up to field managers and operation managers. And in some states, journey workers may apply to be licensed as a master electrician after they have accumulated several more years' experience. Licensing requirements vary by state, and the number of years required may be fewer for those electricians who also have an associate's or bachelor's degree in electrical engineering. But master electricians may advance to supervisory and management-level positions on their way to opening up their own businesses.

What Is the Future Outlook for Electricians?

An electrician is one of those jobs that is directly tied to the economy—when the economy is booming, so is construction, and thus there is an increased need for electricians. The reverse is true as well. When the economy tanks, so does the demand for electricians.

However, electrician jobs are expected to grow by 9 percent through 2026, according to the BLS. That is about average growth and is based on projected increases in the construction industry as well as a growing demand for electricians in alternative power generation. Electricians who have experience installing solar panels should have the best opportunities. Also, electricians who have a range of experience—from electronic systems to industrial wiring—will be very hireable.

There are also many opportunities for women. In an article titled "Is It Difficult to Be a Female Electrician?" on the Electrician Careers Guide website, one expert writes, "You should be able to find training without any difficulty. In fact, you may have an easier time finding an apprenticeship than the men in your area, because trade unions want to employ a diverse workforce, and many actively recruit women and minorities to join."

Find Out More

Electrical Training Alliance
5001 Howerton Way, Suite N
Bowie, MD 20715
website: www.electricaltrainingalliance.org

The Electrical Training Alliance is a collaboration between the National Electrical Contractors Association and the International Brotherhood of Electrical Workers apprenticeship programs. This website includes information on certifications, apprenticeships, journey worker training, and college credits.

ElectricianSchoolEdu.org
website: www.electricianschooledu.org

This educational website includes information on a career as an electrician, including expected salary, schools, journey worker and master's electrician exams, and a state-by-state licensing guide.

Explore the Trades
101 E. Fifth St., Suite 2100
St. Paul, MN 55101
website: https://explorethetrades.org

Explore the Trades offers information on a career as an electrician, including scholarships, apprenticeships, job placements, training, and grants, as well as webinars and quizzes on specific trades.

Independent Electrical Contractors (IEC)
4401 Ford Ave., Suite 1100
Alexandria, VA 22302
website: www.ieci.org

The IEC website offers information for electricians on training, apprenticeships, and safety. The site also features webinars, an industry magazine, and a blog.

National Electrical Contractors Association (NECA)
3 Bethesda Metro Center, Suite 1100
Bethesda, MD 20814
website: www.necanet.org

The NECA is the industry association for the electrical construction industry. Its website includes safety information as well as a learning center, which features career info, webinars, and courses.

Welder

What Does a Welder Do?

Welders bond materials (usually metal) together permanently by using extremely high heat produced by handheld or remote-controlled equipment. They also smooth surfaces and repair holes in metal. Welders sometimes specialize in working with nonmetal materials like plastics and even glass.

It is very precise work. Arc welding, which uses electrical currents to create heat, is the most common type of welding. However, there are more than one hundred different welding processes, depending on the materials welded (what they are made of or how thick they are), the type of welding, whether one is welding joints or flat materials, and the environment in which one is welding. Welders, for example, might work underground building a mine shaft, on land erecting a skyscraper, or underwater repairing a hole in the hull of a ship.

Underwater welding is just one speciality of this profession. Many of these specialists, who need to be certified as a commercial diver, work for offshore oil- and gas-drilling companies repairing

At a Glance

Welder

Minimum Educational Requirements
High school diploma or equivalency

Personal Qualities
Detail oriented, manual dexterity, good eye-hand coordination, physical stamina

Certification and Licensing
Certification recommended but not required

Working Conditions
Long hours on feet or in cramped spaces; various settings, including machine shops, underwater, and underground

Salary Range
About $27,000 to $100,000 or more

Number of Jobs
About 405,000 as of 2016*

Future Job Outlook
Growth of 6 percent through 2026

* Includes welders, cutters, solderers, and brazers

underwater pipes. Allen Garber, chief administrative officer of a Jacksonville, Florida, diving school, says on the Careers in Welding website, "Welding underwater is part of what a commercial diver does. Commercial divers have to find it, clear it, inspect it and repair it or build it new—all in diving gear. It's challenging work, for sure."

Welding cuts across many industries, though most welders work in the manufacturing industry. A welder might work on refrigerators for the manufacturing industry, build airplanes for the military, connect pipes for the oil and gas sector, repair bridges for the government, weld turbine blades for the growing alternative power industry, or create high-powered cars for the racing industry.

Scott Shriver, the chief fabricator for research and development at Hendrick Motorsports, first discovered welding by helping his dad on the family farm. Later he took some high school welding classes and, with encouragement from his teacher, decided to be a welder. Shriver says on Careers in Welding, "I was into racing motorcycles. . . . One day a friend of mine says he wants to race sprint cars—dirttrack-style cars. I helped him build his first car from the chassis up." Shriver says it was not long before he was working for the team behind NASCAR legends like Jeff Gordon and Dale Earnhardt Jr., building cars "from the ground-up."

Being a welder is one of the best-paying jobs among the skilled trades. Mike Rowe, a well-known TV personality and advocate for skilled trades, founded the mikeroweWORKS Foundation, a charity that provides scholarships to students who pursue a career in the skilled trades. On the foundation's website, Rowe lists "fun facts" about potential salaries in the welding profession, including:

> Welding . . . is one of the few jobs where you can earn a six-figure salary with as little as nine months of training!
>
> Underwater welders often charge over $1,000 a day for their services. . . .
>
> Traveling industrial pipe welders earn anywhere between $50,000.00 and $185,000.00 a year.
>
> Military support welders can start at $160,000.00 to more than $200,000.00 a year in the Middle East.

How Do You Become a Welder?

Education

Students who take courses in geometry, mechanical drawing, physics, metallurgy, and chemistry will have a good background for welding. Computer knowledge will also be an advantage. As technology advances in this field, more and more welders will work with computer-controlled machines like robots. A student could also learn basic welding skills through an after-school job in an auto-body shop.

A high school diploma or equivalency along with both technical and on-the-job training is usually required to become a welder. Some employers will hire students without any background and train them. However, most hire entry-level workers who have obtained formal training at a vocational school, community college, or dedicated welding school, and then the company provides more hands-on training. Most welding programs range from six to twelve months. As one expert states on CareerWelder.com, "The major benefit of attending a vocational, trade or technical school is that most programs lead to certifications in various types of welding. Often times they are well known in their local geographic area and employers actively recruit from their programs. It's fairly common for students that attend vocational schools to have job offers before they even graduate."

Apprenticeships and Certification

In addition to certifications for specific processes, the American Welding Society (AWS) offers a Certified Welder certification, which tests welders' knowledge on various procedures for several different industries. It also covers subjects like safety. Although not mandatory, more and more employers are requiring it. And some welding positions, like welders who work in avionics or have specialized techniques, are required to have relevant certifications. Some employers will pay for certification programs for their employees.

Unions often pay for certifications as well. They also offer apprenticeships. Apprenticeships are not mandatory in the welding

Welders use dozens of processes to bond metals and other materials. Welders are in demand in many industries, including aerospace, alternative energy, and manufacturing.

field, but they allow students to earn while they learn and combine on-the-job training with formal classroom instruction. Apprenticeships usually last three or four years, and apprentices normally work full-time while attending classes.

On Careers in Welding, Cajun Seeger, the welding director for an Atlanta union, explains the benefits of doing an apprenticeship: "They get paid to learn." Plus, apprentices obtain college credits for classes they take. And Seeger notes that workers achieve a higher salary upon completion of the apprenticeship program. They get "journeyman's status and journeyman's pay scale."

Skills and Personality

Welding requires specific skills. Welders must be extremely detail oriented. They need to have dexterity, eye-hand coordination, and a steady hand. They also need to have good spatial skills to translate diagrams into 3D objects. And they must be able to use a variety of tools. Some of the tools of the trade include welding magnets and clamps to hold items to be welded together, chipping hammers or metal brushes to clean up welded items, a metal file to smooth rough edges, a band saw to cut through metal, a sheet metal gauge to determine the thickness of metal, and various pliers. Mechanical skills help too when operating high-tech tools like robotic welding equipment. With advances in technology, welding is becoming more and more computerized. For example, robots have been programmed to weld materials using lasers and even explosives. "Welding is not just about working on a manufacturing line anymore," Pennsylvania welding specialist Don Howard says on Careers in Welding.

Welders need to be in good physical shape. Their equipment and materials are heavy, and welders often have to transport items up ladders or onto scaffolding. Sometimes they need to fit into small spaces like an attic or crawl space as well. And welders also stand for long periods performing repetitive movements, sometimes overhead.

On the Job

Employers

The Bureau of Labor Statistics (BLS) groups welders, cutters, solderers, and brazers as one occupational group. This group held close to 405,000 jobs in 2016. Solderers and brazers do similar work to welders except they use different materials with varying melting points. Cutters also work with metal and heat, except they use their skills to cut or dismantle metal items like ships. Five percent of this occupational group identified as self-employed, with 61 percent indicating they were employed by the manufacturing industry. Welders manufacture products from a wide range of industries. For example, welders help manufacture cars, ships, aircraft, boats, rockets, computers, and household appliances. Writer Bethany Cartwright explains on the Alot Careers website, "Welders have skills that are compatible with a number of different industries. The great thing about being a welder is that your specialized skills enable you to jump from industry to industry while you gain valuable experience."

Working Conditions

Work hours for welders vary. Most work full-time shift work plus overtime.

These skilled tradespeople work inside and outside (in all kinds of weather), and in a variety of situations—including underwater. Often welders will work in small, confined areas to limit how far the welding sparks might fly.

According to the BLS, welders have high rates of injuries, one of the highest for all occupations. They sometimes sustain burns from the hot materials they work with, eye injuries from the light generated by their equipment, and lung issues from the toxic fumes they breathe. But strict safety standards and protective gear help limit these injuries in the workplace.

Earnings

The median annual wage for this employment group in May 2017 was almost $40,000, according to the BLS. The lowest-paid 10 percent of these workers earned less than $27,000, and the highest-paid 10 percent earned more than $63,000. According to Careers in Welding, "The starting pay for most welding jobs is pretty basic, especially right out of high school. But, with more experience, the potential to earn two or three times that amount is definitely there. And making $100,000 or more isn't out of the question. But only if you are the best of the best."

Opportunities for Advancement

The best way to advance in welding is to obtain as much training and certifications in as many different welding processes as possible. The more one knows, the more valuable one will be to an employer. Plus, obtaining an AWS-certified welder designation can lead to more opportunities and a higher salary.

What Is the Future Outlook for Welders?

The BLS reports that growth for this employment group will be average (6 percent) through 2026. That should translate into about 22,500 more jobs. The growth reflects the pool of professionals who will be retiring in the coming years, the demand to build or repair aging infrastructure across the United States, and the growing alternative power industry.

Welding is one of those professions that is needed in many industries. That translates into job security. According to the BLS's *Occupational Outlook Handbook*:

> Employment growth reflects the need for welders in manufacturing because of the importance and versatility of welding as a manufacturing process. The basic skills of welding are similar across industries, so welders can easily shift from one industry to another, depending on where they are needed most. For example, welders who are laid off in the automotive manufacturing industry may be able to find work in the oil and gas industry.

And prospects for female welders have never been better, according to an editorial on the AWS website. Monica Pfarr, the executive director of the AWS Foundation, writes:

> Women proved their ability to handle tough construction and manufacturing jobs in filling labor shortages during World War II. Now, with the need for skilled welders again at a premium, many employers are specifically seeking women as a means of creating gender diversity in the workplace. Welding provides relatively high average pay, and there is typically little or no gap between male and female salaries in this field.

Find Out More

American Welding Society (AWS)
8669 NW Thirty-Sixth St., #130
Miami, FL 33166
website: www.aws.org

The AWS offers up-to-date information on the welding industry, including certification, volunteer opportunities, scholarships, online training, industry updates, and career opportunities. The AWS website also has a blog, career path information, and industry videos.

CareerOneStop
website: www.careeronestop.org

CareerOneStop is a one-stop website sponsored by the US Department of Labor. This informative site features training information, industry resources such as videos, and state licensing requirements. There is also a career and ability skill assessment to see whether a person is a good fit for a particular career path.

Careers in Welding
website: www.careersinwelding.com

Careers in Welding is a web portal collaboration between the AWS and the National Center for Welding Education and Training. The site features resources for students considering a career in welding, including information on AWS certification, jobs, educational opportunities, certification, and seminars.

mikeroweWORKS Foundation
website: http://profoundlydisconnected.com

The mikeroweWORKS Foundation is a nonprofit public charity that helps train people for skilled jobs through its scholarship programs. Resources on its website include scholarship information as well as state-by-state information on apprenticeships, industry associations, education, and financial aid.

US Department of Labor (DOL)
200 Constitution Ave. NW
Washington, DC 20210
website: www.dol.gov

The DOL website offers information on apprenticeship programs for all trades as well a job finder and career center.

Automotive Technician

At a Glance

Automotive Technician

Minimum Educational Requirements
High school diploma or equivalency

Personal Qualities
Good customer-service skills, mechanical abilities, manual dexterity, physical strength and stamina

Certification
National Institute for Automotive Service Excellence certification encouraged

Working Conditions
Usually indoors but often in hot (or cold) service bays; on feet for long periods, dirty and greasy

Salary Range
About $22,000 to $66,000 or more

Number of Jobs
Almost 750,000 as of 2016

Future Job Outlook
Growth of 6 percent through 2026

What Does an Automotive Technician Do?

Between 2017 and 2018, 17.5 million new cars were sold in the United States—adding to the more than 270 million vehicles already on the road. With that many cars, the potential for something to go wrong is high. When car brakes fail, a check engine light comes on, a car develops an oil leak, or there is a nationwide airbag recall, somebody has to take care of those problems. That somebody is usually an automotive technician.

Automotive technicians, also called mechanics, inspect, maintain, and repair cars and light trucks. They are trained to keep cars in good working order, diagnose problems, and fix those problems. They also must be skilled in using a wide variety of hand and power tools, most of which they are expected to buy themselves. This can run into thousands of dollars. Those who work in auto shops usually have access to equipment like computerized diagnostic tools, welding tools, and hoists.

Some automotive technicians are generalists; others specialize. Specialties might include transmissions, brakes, diagnostics, auto body, restoration, or wheel alignment. And a usual day for a technician might include everything from changing a car's oil to installing new tires to replacing a car's braking system. In *U.S. News & World Report*'s "Best Jobs Rankings" for 2018, Diane Larson, owner of an auto repair shop in Peabody, Massachusetts, confirms that an automotive technician's job is never the same two days in a row: "Each day typically brings them some type of surprise or challenge, whether it be finding a water pump . . . that was leaking or [addressing] rust problems."

Traditionally, automotive technicians work on mechanical systems, but as cars change and evolve technologically, so do the jobs of the people who work on them. These days a mechanic's duties might include working on computer-controlled electronic systems like accident-avoidance sensors or braking, transmission, and steering systems. These increasingly complex systems are part of the reason these tradespeople are now more often called technicians than mechanics. Larson acknowledges that the mechanic's trade has become "increasingly technological" over the years. "Our industry now involves fixing computers. We used to be able to fix cars with wrenches. Now we're fixing multi-computer systems [like GPS]."

Currently, there is a growing need for modern-day automotive technicians who can service hybrid and alternative fuel vehicles (AFVs), cars that run on electricity or solar power, for example. Increasingly, automotive technicians will need to know the fundamentals of AFVs, including how they are designed and how to diagnose and fix any issues they might have.

Automotive technicians get into the business for a variety of reasons. Some have a passion for cars. Others enjoy working with machinery. Still others see it as a stable career. Says one expert on the Automotive Training Centres website:

For some people, wanting to become a mechanic is a dream they've had since childhood. They might have nostalgic memories of watching family members work on cars and have always dreamed of getting under the hood themselves. Some people may have developed their love for cars in their teen years, when they became old enough to drive. Others may just be mechanically inclined and have always been hands-on and curious about how engines work.

If you see yourself in any or all of these examples, you're probably meant for an auto mechanic career!

How Do You Become an Automotive Technician?

Education

High school courses in automotive repair, electronics, computers, and math can provide a great start for a student looking to have a career as an automotive technician. However, most employers prefer to hire people who have completed a training program in automotive technology.

These programs are available at community colleges and vocational schools and will require a high school diploma or equivalency. They generally last from six months to two years and include formal education as well as hands-on training. Courses might include everything from basic electrical fundamentals to engine performance, brake and climate control systems, and manual and automatic transmissions.

Obtaining an associate's degree is another option, which would include a mix of formal courses as well as on-the-job training. Some associate's degree programs are sponsored by automobile manufacturers and car dealerships. Students enrolled in these programs often attend classes in the evening and work full-time in a repair shop under a technician's supervision.

It is possible to get an entry-level position at an auto shop without postsecondary education. Trainee technicians and technicians' helpers are sometimes hired right out of high school, learn on the job, and work their way up.

Automotive technicians must upgrade their education from time to time to stay on top of industry changes and the ever-evolving technology. Employees can also take short-term certificate programs in specialty subjects such as brake maintenance or air-conditioning to make themselves more valuable to an employer. And automotive technicians who wish to start their own garage should take some business courses.

With the push to be greener, there are programs available for people who would like to specialize in working on hybrids or AFVs. Courses might include hybrid fuel technology, power electronics for electric or hybrid vehicles, and even how to convert a standard vehicle to an AFV.

Certification

An automotive technician may get certified by the National Institute for Automotive Service Excellence (ASE), a standard that many employers require as a condition of employment. The ASE tests a technician's competence in each of the following nine specialty areas: brakes; automatic transmission/transaxle; electrical/electronic systems; engine performance; engine repair; heating and air-conditioning; manual drive train and axles; suspension and steering; and light vehicle diesel engines. The certification tests are approximately fifty questions in multiple-choice format and generally take one to two hours. Various test preparation resources can be found online.

Technicians must have a minimum of two years' experience (or combination of education and experience) and pass the exam to be ASE-certified. To retain ASE certification status, an automotive technician must be retested every five years, although the retests are much shorter. And any or all of these certifications would positively affect a technician's pay. Technicians who obtain certification in the first eight specialty areas may achieve ASE Master

Technician status, which would definitely expand an automotive technician's opportunities and salary range.

Newly hired automotive technicians are required to obtain industry certification in proper refrigerant handling from the US Environmental Protection Agency (EPA). Many trade schools, unions, and industry associations offer training programs to help with the EPA exam.

Skills and Personality

Mechanical aptitude, electronic and technical skills, and familiarity with a variety of tools are some of the qualities and skills needed for automotive technician jobs. Technicians also need to have good eye-hand coordination and manual dexterity. Being detail oriented is important as well because there are so many parts to an automobile. Technicians also need physical strength because sometimes they need to lift heavy car parts like wheels or axles.

Also, automotive technicians who work in small shops or own their own shop need great customer-service skills, since dealing with customers is a big part of their job. Talking to customers and listening to what they need is how an automotive shop and its technicians build their business, loyalty, and reputation.

And finally, automotive technicians need problem-solving skills. A 2016 article on the Advanced Technology Institute website called "4 Reasons Being a Mechanic Could Be an Amazing Life Choice" explains, "Sure, you may change a lot of oil, but you can also work on novel challenges including race cars, classic cars and heavy equipment. . . . On the same day in a repair shop, you can work on vehicles made 40 years ago and ones made last month. Each car presents new dilemmas needing your talent and skill."

Employers

According to the Bureau of Labor Statistics (BLS), there were almost 750,000 automotive technicians in 2016. These tradespeople were employed at gas stations, auto parts stores, accessories stores, and tire stores (9 percent); auto repair shops (27 percent); and car dealerships (31 percent). In addition, 13 percent identified as being self-employed.

Working Conditions

The majority of technicians work full-time. Depending on where they work, some are required to work evenings and weekends as well as overtime. Self-employed technicians have more flexibility to set their own hours.

Being an automotive technician can be physically demanding. Technicians spend a lot of time on their feet. They also are in awkward positions looking under hoods or lying under cars for long periods of time.

Garages tend to be dirty places to work. Grime is a daily issue, and automotive technicians deal with a lot of greasy parts and tools.

Workplace injuries are common with technicians. They have one of the highest rates of injuries in all occupations. Most, however, are minor injuries like sprains, cuts, and bruises.

Earnings

U.S. News & World Report's "Best Jobs Rankings" lists automotive mechanics as the number four best maintenance and repair job for 2018. The rankings are based on findings like job stress, future job prospects, and of course, salary.

The BLS puts the median annual wage for automotive technicians at $39,550 in May 2017. The lowest-paid 10 percent earned less than $22,610, and the highest-paid 10 percent earned more than $65,430.

Automotive technicians who worked for dealerships on average earned the highest salaries, about $43,000 annually. Those who worked at auto parts, accessories, and tire stores earned amounts in the lower range of income.

Automotive technicians are compensated in various ways: by the hour, by commission, or on a flat-rate, per item basis (a predetermined amount for each type of service). ASE-certified technicians generally earn more than their noncertified counterparts.

Opportunities for Advancement

Having formal postsecondary training, ASE certifications, or a Master Mechanic designation would definitely boost an automotive technician's opportunities for advancement in this industry. Those technicians who have great skills in the garage, as well as out front with the customers, will advance faster as well—and perhaps all the way to management positions. And of course, some automotive technicians advance to management positions by choosing to open their own shops.

> ### What Is the Future Outlook for Automotive Technicians?

The BLS reports that automotive technician jobs will grow by 6 percent through 2026. That is considered average growth, but it will still result in almost forty-eight thousand new jobs. Many of these jobs will be needed to replace current technicians who are retiring or leaving the industry, meaning automotive technicians will always be in demand. Overall, the automotive repair industry has a fairly stable future. As one expert on the Automotive Training Centres website states, "Entering a career as a mechanic means guaranteeing a future of steady work. Slumps in the economy can affect consumers buying new cars, but vehicles will always require maintenance and repair. Changes that may disrupt other businesses have very little effect on the automotive service industry, so there's really no such thing as a slow season for auto mechanics."

Of course, the industry is changing. With more technological advances, no one can really predict the future. But even a self-driving car will need maintenance.

Find Out More

Automotive Service Association (ASA)
8209 Mid Cities Blvd.
North Richland Hills, TX 76182
website: https://asashop.org

The ASA is a leading organization in the auto repair industry. Its website offers students a job board, internship information, and various resources, including a career center.

Automotive Youth Educational Systems (AYES)
101 Blue Seal Dr. SE, Suite 101
Leesburg, VA 20175
website: www.nada.org/ayes

AYES is a national collaboration of automobile manufacturers, car dealerships, and educational departments working together to prepare students for entry-level positions in dealerships with openings nationwide. The website offers information on job shadowing opportunities, internships, scholarships, and job placements.

CareerOneStop
website: www.careeronestop.org

CareerOneStop is a one-stop website sponsored by the US Department of Labor. This informative site features training information, industry resources such as videos, and state licensing requirements. There is also a career and skill assessment to see whether a person is a good fit for a particular career path.

National Institute for Automotive Service Excellence (ASE) Education Foundation
1503 Edwards Ferry Rd. NE, Suite 401
Leesburg, VA 20176
website: www.asealliance.org

The ASE offers program accreditation, student career development, and ASE student certification information. The ASE website features various resources on subjects like scholarships.

Solar Photovoltaic Installer

What Does a Solar Photovoltaic Installer Do?

Solar photovoltaic installers, also called PV installers, assemble, install, and maintain solar panels on the rooftops of homes and commercial buildings. PV installers may also work with customers to configure solar panel systems to collect sunlight. An inverter then converts the sunlight from a direct current to an alternating current so it can be used to generate electricity. Installers also design and install PV systems for solar farms, which are large-scale rows of PV panels on the ground that collect and generate electricity for thousands of homes and buildings at one time.

Being a PV installer is hard work. It requires heavy lifting. And because the large panels need structural support, a PV installer often constructs frames in accordance with building codes. Installers, who work in teams, also apply weather sealant around the panels. And depending on state laws, sometimes installers connect the panels to the electrical grid.

At a Glance

Solar Photovoltaic Installer

Minimum Educational Requirements
High school diploma or equivalency

Personal Qualities
Physical stamina, mechanical abilities, detail oriented

Apprenticeship and Certification
Optional

Working Conditions
Primarily outdoors on roofs; sometimes indoors in tight spaces

Salary Range
Average of $28,000 to more than $61,000

Number of Jobs
Over 11,000 as of 2016

Future Job Outlook
Growth of 105 percent through 2026

PV installer jobs are part of a rapidly growing industry. The Office of Energy Efficiency & Renewable Energy says on its website, "The solar energy industry is booming. Since 2008, the amount of solar energy connected to the grid has increased more than 20 fold. . . . This expansion has resulted in the creation of thousands of new solar industry jobs. . . . Solar is the next great American industry."

Because this is a relatively new industry, and one that is dependent on locations that receive a fair amount of sun, PV installer jobs are currently concentrated in a handful of areas. The author of *Ditch the Desk: The Complete E-book to Starting a Career in Solar Energy* puts this in perspective: "There are more solar energy workers in California than there are actors; more solar energy workers in Texas than there are ranchers; and nationwide, there are more solar energy workers than there are coal miners."

A career as a PV installer will appeal to those who like to work outside and who want to do something that can make a difference in the world. *Ditch the Desk*, a publication of the Ecotech Institute, explains:

> Many solar technicians have decided they'd rather do anything else but sit inside a cubicle for a large part of their day. Some have chosen the industry to make a green, clean difference in current energy usage, or others want a more fulfilling career path—either way, they are the kind of people who like to mix it up, problem solve and stay on their toes. . . . In the solar energy industry, a technician will find themselves outside in the fresh air and sunshine, always presented with new challenges and opportunities to lead.

How Do You Become a Solar PV Installer?

Education

Because solar energy is a relatively new industry, formal educational programs for PV installers might be a challenge to find, depending on where one lives. This means some employers will take students with a high school diploma (or equivalency) and

Solar photovoltaic installers put rooftop solar panels in place. Their work includes assembling, installing, and maintaining rooftop solar panels.

provide on-the-job training. Training could take anywhere from a month to a year.

The technical school and community college programs that do exist vary in length by state and generally last a few days to several months. Courses include panel installation techniques, solar system design, and safety training. These courses are often available online.

Experience in construction, particularly in roofing or electrical work, can both boost job prospects and shorten training time. Students may also receive training from solar PV system manufacturers, who sometimes provide training on their specific products.

A quick look at some current job postings for solar PV installers shows the range of qualifications required. A company hiring for a position in Southern California prefers someone with experience with hand tools and who can take accurate measurements. A background in construction is preferred but not required, and solar or electrical experience would be considered a plus. Another job posting, this one for a solar PV installer in Maryland, specifies a preference for someone who has completed a two-year trade school program or has reached the level of journey worker electrician.

Constance Odle, a former production manager for graphic and industrial designers, knew nothing about PV installation when she started out. With only a desire to break into the green sector, she sent an application to a solar electricity company based in Oakland, California. The company not only hired her but gave her the training she needed. Today she manages a group of PV installers and believes the industry is still new enough that other companies might be willing to take a chance on people without experience. In *U.S. News and World Report*'s "Best Jobs Rankings," Odle says, "They're not all necessarily looking for people with solar backgrounds."

Apprenticeships and Certification

Some PV installers learn the job as part of an apprenticeship, particularly electricians and roofing apprentices. Many new installers start out by building the support structures for the PV panels. They might also perform the basic installation of the panels, leaving the electrical hookup to more experienced PV installers.

There are currently no standard certification programs for PV installers. However, any certifications an installer might obtain may increase his or her job opportunities.

Skills and Personality

A PV installer needs many skills. Good communication skills are a must. Installers need to communicate effectively with clients as well as other workers (particularly on construction sites) to ensure that proper safety and installation procedures are followed. It is also important that PV installers be detail oriented. Installation instructions need to be followed precisely or the PV system may not work properly. Good mechanical skills are also a necessity since this is a hands-on job with complex electrical and mechanical systems. Standard tools used by PV installers include saws, power drills, wrenches, and screwdrivers, among others.

Physical stamina is also crucial for PV installers. This is an extremely physical job, and installers are often on their feet all day. Plus, they routinely carry heavy equipment and materials weighing up to 50 pounds (22.7 kg) up and down ladders.

On the Job

Employers
According to the Bureau of Labor Statistics (BLS), installation made up the largest share of the solar power jobs in 2017, at 52 percent. And in 2016 PV installers held approximately 11,300 jobs. The largest employer of PV installers were plumbing, heating, and air-conditioning contractors, at 43 percent. About 20 percent of PV installers were employed by electricians, with about another 20 percent identifying as self-employed.

Working Conditions
Working conditions for PV installers can be challenging. They lift extremely heavy loads and work primarily on rooftops. So this job is not ideal for anyone with a fear of heights. In addition, the bulk of the work is done outdoors (often in the hot sun); however, installers sometimes need to work in attics or crawl spaces to connect the PV panels to the electrical grid. So someone with claustrophobia may want to consider a different occupation or perhaps consider working at ground level, building solar farms.

Injuries are not uncommon in this field. Solar PV installers sometimes receive minor cuts while building support structures. They also sometimes get burned by touching hot panels. But the majority of injuries in this field result from falls from ladders or roofs, as well as electrical shocks sustained while connecting panels to the electrical grid system.

PV installers mostly work a regular nine-to-five, Monday-through-Friday workweek. Overtime may be required for emergencies or when working on a construction project that is behind schedule.

Job location may be an issue as well. A person who wishes to be a PV installer may have to move to a state that has a thriving solar energy industry. California, for instance, has the nation's largest concentration of solar energy projects.

Despite all of this, there are tangible rewards connected with being a PV installer. Odle talks about job satisfaction in this growing field: "Seeing a project completed is rewarding. . . . It's really satisfying to see that—to know that it's going to help the planet for 50 years."

Earnings

The BLS puts the median annual wage for solar PV installers at $39,490 as of May 2017. The lowest-paid 10 percent in this industry earned around $28,000, and the highest-paid 10 percent earned more than $61,000.

Opportunities for Advancement

PV installers who have completed a photovoltaic systems program will have the best opportunities to move up in this industry. Installers with certifications will do well, too. And anyone with electrical, carpentry, roofing, or construction experience will also have more opportunities in this up-and-coming industry.

> ### What Is the Future Outlook for Solar PV Installers?

PV installers are listed as the number one fastest-growing occupation on the BLS website. They are projected to have the highest percentage of employment growth of all other occupations through 2026. In fact, PV installer employment is projected to grow 105 percent. This will translate into almost twelve thousand new jobs.

State and federal actions may affect the continued growth of this industry. On the one hand, many states and municipalities have offered incentives like tax rebates and subsidies to encourage home and business owners to adopt solar energy. And in May 2018 California became the first state to require all new homes to be built with solar panels—effective in 2020. These actions could hasten industry growth and lead to more jobs for PV installers. On the other hand, new tariffs imposed by the federal government may result in slower growth and fewer new jobs.

Whichever way the political winds blow, many observers believe that over the long haul the solar industry will remain strong.

Writer Veronica Wright on the *Pick My Solar* blog calls the growth of the solar energy industry "practically exponential"—particularly for PV installers. In a June 2017 blog post titled "5 Reasons to Consider a Career in the Solar Industry," she writes:

> Strong growth is also expected in other jobs that are relevant to the solar industry; making unexpected layoffs unlikely. As more and more families and businesses begin to use solar energy, growth will continue. . . .
>
> One thing that people often overlook is the importance of morale and job satisfaction . . . being proud of what you do, and feeling as if your work contributes to the greater good.
>
> When you work in the solar energy field, the work you do contributes to overall improvements to the environment including reducing pollution and beating back climate change. . . .
>
> In addition to that, the installation of commercial and residential solar panels can result in massive savings. . . . These savings can contribute nicely to the overall economic development of communities and result in more jobs. . . .
>
> The level of growth in this industry is nothing short of spectacular, and the future looks extraordinarily bright.

All of this is great news for anyone looking to enter a career as a solar PV installer.

Find Out More

Ecotech Institute
1400 S. Abilene St.
Aurora, CO 80012
website: www.ecotechinstitute.com

The Ecotech Institute offers training for solar PV installers as well as career information and industry updates.

Interstate Renewable Energy Council (IREC)
PO Box 1156
Latham, NY 12110
website: https://irecusa.org

The IREC is an independent not-for-profit organization. Its website features certification information, training programs, and a career video series.

Office of Energy Efficiency & Renewable Energy (EERE)
Forrestal Building
1000 Independence Ave. SW
Washington, DC 20585
website: www.energy.gov/eere

The EERE's mission is to create American leadership in the transition to a clean energy economy worldwide. Its website provides training programs, internships, industry education, and career information in the solar industry.

Roof Integrated Solar Energy (RISE)
10255 W. Higgins Rd., Suite 600
Rosemont, IL 60018
website: www.riseprofessional.org

RISE offers webinars and industry literature as well as the Certified Solar Roofing Professional (CSRP) credential program for solar PV installers.

Solar Energy International (SEI)
SEI Training Facility
39845 Mathews Ln.
Paonia, CO 81428
website: www.solarenergy.org

The SEI has been around for two decades and offers classroom, hands-on, and online training and certification in both residential and commercial photovoltaic systems. Its website also provides career information and job boards.

Wind Turbine Technician

What Does a Wind Turbine Technician Do?

A wind turbine technician installs, maintains, and repairs wind turbines—towers of more than 300 feet (91 m) that have rotating blades and convert wind energy into electricity. Turbines are monitored electronically twenty-four hours a day, and wind turbine technicians are responsible for keeping these extremely complex structures running efficiently.

Most of a wind turbine technician's time is spent ascending several turbines a day to inspect them. Safely attached with a harness, technicians climb up and down on a ladder located inside the tower. Some towers have a climb-assist system (like a motorized chairlift) that propels technicians up and down the tower much faster. And sometimes technicians must ascend the tower on the outside using ropes.

The bulk of a wind turbine technician's work takes place in the nacelle, the small compartment at the top of the tower where the

At a Glance

Wind Turbine Technician

Minimum Educational Requirements
Community college or technical school program

Personal Qualities
Problem-solving skills, detail oriented, physical stamina

Certification
Optional

Working Conditions
Sometimes outdoors, often in tight, confined spaces at great heights

Salary Range
About $38,000 to $80,000

Number of Jobs
Almost 6,000 as of 2016

Future Job Outlook
Growth of 96 percent through 2026

gears and electronics are housed. Technicians often do preventive maintenance and testing on the turbine's electrical, mechanical, and hydraulic systems. Technicians must inspect every inch of the turbine—inside and out—from the turbine blades at the top of the structure to the transmission systems located underground. To do this, technicians use various hand tools and power tools as well as electrical and wind-measuring devices.

Wind turbine technicians need to stay ahead of any potential problems, because an offline turbine translates into lost energy and lost money. Any issues found are reported and scheduled for repair. Technicians also collect the recorded turbine data (wind speed and direction) from the sensors mounted on the nacelle as well—all this from hundreds of feet above the ground.

Jessica Kilroy is a wind turbine technician who was featured on the Weather Channel's *That's Amazing.* In "The Wind Climber" episode, she says, "You're basically doing construction work on ropes. Most people think, 'God, you're insane. That's totally dangerous.' But actually it's statistically safer than driving to work."

Kilroy, who is also a rock climber, compares climbing rocks to climbing turbines: "Rock climbing and blade repair require the same skills. Being able to have no fear of heights, be comfortable in ropes as well as being able to figure out how to get yourself out of a weird situation." A "weird situation" could include wind whipping around the top of the turbine while the technician is up there trying to repair damage caused by a lightning strike. Turbines are susceptible to strikes because they are usually the highest structure in an area. If a blade is damaged during a storm, a technician has to climb up the outside of the tower to fix it. Kilroy continues, "We repair the fiberglass using grinders and sanders. . . . It's really similar to surf board repair except there's 350 feet of nothingness beneath me. You're on a blade and you're straddling it and the wind is bucking you around." Kilroy likens it to riding a bull in a rodeo—all in a day's work for a wind turbine technician.

How Do You Become a Wind Turbine Technician?

Education

Students interested in becoming wind turbine technicians should look for community colleges and technical schools with programs in wind turbine maintenance or wind energy technology. A high school diploma or equivalency is required to enroll in these programs.

Both the one-year certificate and the two-year associate's degree programs offer courses with subjects such as turbine design, maintenance, and repair; mechanical, electrical, and hydraulic systems; electricity; circuitry; and safety. However, the associate's degree will also provide hands-on training that allows students to work on actual turbines.

Another option to consider is an associate's degree in applied science. It is best to find a program that is specific to wind energy, if possible.

Training and Certification

Most wind turbine technicians learn on the job. According to WindTurbineTechnicians.net, "The good news is this field is growing by leaps and bounds, so you should have no problem finding a job. . . . The bad news is you will need substantial training to understand all aspects of the technology and safely carry out the job . . . yet . . . most wind turbine technicians are partially trained on the job."

Wind turbine technicians typically receive about twelve months of training related to the specific wind turbines they will service. Part of this training may be by the manufacturer, and sometimes wind turbine servicing contractors offer internships. Training covers everything from building a wind turbine to electrical safety to first aid and tower rescue. "Being safe on the job is THE number one priority," according to *Ditch the Desk: The Complete E-book to Starting a Career in Wind Energy*.

Professional certification is not mandatory in this field. However, having certifications in some of these key areas, like safety, may give a prospective employee an edge over the competition. Auston Van Slyke, program director of the Wind Energy Technology program at the Ecotech Institute in Aurora, Colorado, agrees. "Graduates of [accredited degree] programs gain skills in addition to technical skills that help them get promotions much faster. . . . It's pretty easy to find jobs these days as the profession is growing rapidly."

Skills and Personality

Wind turbine technicians need to be physically fit. They must be capable of climbing ladders that are at least 300 feet (91 m) high with tools and equipment that weigh close to 50 pounds (22.7 kg) — several times a day.

It helps if turbine technicians are mechanically inclined. Experience in automotive mechanics or electronics is an asset. Having a working knowledge of circuit boards and computers helps too, because computers are used to monitor electrical activity.

Wind turbine technicians need a couple of other capabilities, too. It helps if they are detail oriented, because they need to maintain precise service records and take exact measurements. They also need to be effective communicators to perform their duties both safely and effectively when working with others.

On the Job

Employers

Wind turbine technicians held about 5,800 jobs in 2016. According to the Bureau of Labor Statistics (BLS), 31 percent of wind turbine technicians were employed by electric power generation firms, 23 percent worked in repair and maintenance, and 17 percent identified as self-employed. Wind turbine technician jobs are found in many parts of the United States. According to *Ditch the Desk*, "Most wind jobs are in the Midwest, Southwest and North-east regions of the U.S. Texas, Iowa and California lead all states in wind power generating capacity, but other states, like Illinois, Indiana, Oregon and Washington are in the process of majorly increasing their capacity."

Working Conditions

Wind turbine technicians need to travel to the wind turbine farms, which are usually located in remote areas. And although wind turbine technicians sometimes service underground transmission systems and field substations, the majority of their work is aboveground. These professionals cannot have a fear of heights or of small spaces, because wind turbine technicians primarily work in the turbine's nacelle. Van Slyke explains, "Fear of heights is something everyone deals with at some level. Most new technicians get over it." *U.S. News & World Report* describes a typical workday this way:

> Windtechs will likely meet at an operational or maintenance building, where they'll learn from their manager about the type of task they'll need to perform. . . . Then, in groups of two or three, they'll take work trucks, which they've loaded with all of their gear, and drive out to the wind farm. Once there, they'll climb up the side of the wind turbine, which usually takes eight minutes or so, to a room inside the turbine, where they'll do their work for the day.

Wind turbine technicians also have to deal with extreme weather conditions and temperatures—sometimes while dangling from the outside of a tower. But even though the job can be dangerous, it has its benefits. Van Slyke explains, "The big picture of what you're doing—renewable energy--is rewarding. You're making the world more environmentally friendly."

Although most wind turbine technicians work regular work hours, they may be called to emergencies at night or on weekends. Technicians may work at more than one site, and some are required to live in remote areas. In *Ditch the Desk*, Paul Roamer, president of a Colorado-based company that provides services to the wind industry, shares what he looks for in a prospective job candidate:

> Right now I have a crew in the Bahamas, a crew in Alaska, a crew in Kansas—we're all over the place. If you're willing to be flexible, open to new opportunities—travel and see the country while you're doing it—learn lots of different things, and be challenged along the way, it's a great fit. If you want to know what you'll be doing tomorrow, then you're in the wrong place. If you're not willing to put up with travel or working outside in all kinds of weather and getting your hands dirty, I don't think that this is the right field for you.

Earnings

The BLS lists the median annual wage for a wind turbine technician at almost $54,000 in May 2017. The lowest-paid 10 percent in this job earned less than $38,000, and the highest-paid 10 percent earned more than $80,000. Wind turbine technicians who made the highest salaries worked primarily for electric power generation plants. Generally, the more experience one has, the higher the salary. Geographical location may also affect a wind turbine technician's salary. According to WindTurbineTechnicians.net, "Many companies will adjust their compensation based on the cost of living in the area. Also worth noting—a traveling Wind Turbine Technician can earn more, because of their mobility and willingness to go where the wind farms are."

Opportunities for Advancement

Because there are currently no required certifications for wind turbine technicians, any extra training or courses will be a definite advantage for advancing in this career.

What Is the Future Outlook for Wind Turbine Technicians?

The BLS reports that a wind turbine technician is the number two fastest-growing occupation of all occupations (behind solar photovoltaic installers), with a projected increase of employment through 2026. Wind turbine technician jobs are expected to grow by 96 percent, an increase of almost six thousand jobs.

"Industry sources report that there is a current shortage of trained wind technicians," according to *Ditch the Desk*. This shortage, the increased demand for wind technology, and the growing interest in offshore wind turbines (which are located in oceans rather than on land) all bode well for future job growth. According to *Ditch the Desk*:

> As long as the wind keeps on blowing, we'll have a tremendous resource for electricity. And, more and more people are realizing the importance of investing in this energy, making wind power cheaper and pushing those in the industry to make it more efficient. From the existing land-based wind farms to the future of offshore wind technology, the future of the industry is strong.

Find Out More

American Wind Energy Association (AWEA)
1501 M St. NW, 10th Floor
Washington, DC 20005
website: www.awea.org

The AWEA offers webinars, blog posts, industry networking opportunities, a wind energy community forum, and a resource library. An interactive map database for members shows all current and upcoming wind projects in the United States.

Ecotech Institute
1400 S. Abilene St.
Aurora, CO 80012
website: www.ecotechinstitute.com

The Ecotech Institute offers training for wind energy workers as well as career information and industry updates.

Occupational Information Network (O*NET) Online
website: www.onetonline.org

O*NET offers a comprehensive database of occupational information on close to one thousand occupations. O*NET assists people nationwide in finding the training and jobs they need, as well as connecting employers to skilled workers. Career exploration tools and links to jobs, training, apprenticeships, and credentials are featured on this site.

Office of Energy Efficiency & Renewable Energy (EERE)
Forrestal Building
1000 Independence Ave. SW
Washington, DC 20585
website: www.energy.gov/eere

The EERE's mission is to create American leadership in the transition to a clean energy economy worldwide. Its website provides training programs, internships, industry education, and career information in the wind industry.

WindTurbineTechnicians.net
website: www.windturbinetechnicians.net

This website is a one-stop shop for all things related to having a career as a wind turbine technician, including industry information, schools, training, and job listings.

Chef

What Does a Chef Do?

A chef's job entails much more than just creating and presenting fabulous food. On a typical day a chef, sometimes known as an executive chef or head cook, plans the day's menu. The chef must estimate what ingredients are needed and make sure all items are available and ordered. The chef also needs to ensure that safety and sanitation standards are being met or perhaps inspect a food order for quality and freshness. Then there is the paperwork. The chef is responsible for staff scheduling, budgets, and promoting the restaurant. And all of that is in addition to training staff on how to prepare new recipes and overseeing the preparation of the food by the sous chef (the chef's second in command) and the other cooks. In other words, the chef is the boss. Chefs actually do very little cooking. People interested in a culinary career but without the duties of a boss, may train as a sous chef, one of the most sought-after jobs on the line, as they call it. The "line" is literally a line of cooks (called line cooks) who work side by side in a restaurant kitchen each with their own duties. A line cook

At a Glance

Chef

Minimum Educational Requirements
High school diploma or equivalency

Personal Qualities
Creative, physical stamina, eye-hand coordination, manual dexterity, detail oriented, excellent people skills

Certification and Licensing
Optional certifications; some states require occupational licenses

Working Conditions
Long hours on feet, hot kitchens and sharp utensils, high stress, fast pace

Salary Range
About $25,000 to $78,000

Number of Jobs
About 147,000 as of 2016

Future Job Outlook
Growth of 10 percent through 2026

A chef adds the finishing touches to plates that will be delivered to diners. Some chefs do a lot of cooking while others do more menu planning and purchasing and still others do both.

might prep food, chop vegetables, or work on the grill. Or perhaps they might specialize as a baker, chocolatier, sushi chef, or pastry chef—all of whom work under the head chef.

Chefs who run catering businesses face similar issues as chefs who work in restaurants. They may not be part of the intense hierarchy of a commercial kitchen, but they will still spend more time running the kitchen than actually cooking.

People who prefer independence as well as spending most of their time creating meals might consider a career as a private or personal chef. A private chef works for one client, usually as a full-time employee, whereas a personal chef may work for many different clients.

Chef and cookbook author Emily Ellyn shares what it takes to be a chef on the *We Are Chefs* blog, sponsored by the American Culinary Federation. In a 2017 article, she offers advice to aspiring chefs:

> Are you ready to work hard? Work long hours with little money? Are you ready to work in extreme conditions where you are burned, cut and yelled at while working to create amazing food?

If so, you'll experience instant gratification, more so than possibly any other job. Through it all you'll experience the closest friendships ever bound by a love of the craft, sweat and tears!

She encourages culinary students to be open to various opportunities in a wide-ranging industry: "Work in the areas of business you are interested in and those you would not think to pursue. You never know, you may become a corporate chef or restaurant owner; a food photographer or food critic; or maybe even a line cook on a cruise ship or an educator!"

How Do You Become a Chef?

Education

There are no educational requirements to be a chef, and the majority of chefs learn on the job. Generally, aspiring chefs start out as a dishwasher or a prep cook cutting or peeling vegetables in a restaurant. Depending on their skills and talents, they could move up to a line cook, an assistant chef, and eventually, a sous chef.

Some enroll in culinary programs at a community college, technical school, or culinary arts school. A high school diploma or equivalency is required for these options. The most cost-effective way to obtain a culinary education is a community college, where a student can get a certificate, a diploma, an associate's degree, or even a bachelor's degree in culinary arts. This can take anywhere from one to four years. Classes include cooking, creating menus, food safety, inventory control, kitchen sanitation, and the procurement of supplies. A trade school is often the fastest way to obtain culinary skills. Some schools offer training while a student is still in high school, which may help in obtaining a job. The most expensive route to becoming a chef is a formal culinary arts school. These bachelor's degrees include courses in restaurant management and marketing, as well as in international cuisine such as French cooking.

Formal education is definitely an advantage, though most likely a person will still have to start at the bottom. Hands-on experience working under various cooks and chefs will teach prospective chefs many of the same skills they might learn at a school, plus they will learn how a kitchen works.

Skills and experience are what counts, according to the Learn How to Become website. The site explains that it is a long road to becoming a chef: "It requires countless hours of hard work, especially in the early years. 'Paying your dues' is definitely what aspiring chefs must do to reach the upper ranks of the profession."

Apprenticeships and Certification

There are very few apprenticeship programs for chefs. All require a high school diploma or equivalency as well as being a minimum age of seventeen. Apprenticeships, which are generally two years, provide both formal classes and on-the-job training. They are usually sponsored by professional culinary institutions, industry associations, trade unions, or the armed forces.

Apprentices typically receive about two thousand hours per year under a chef's supervision. Courses cover food sanitation and safety, basic knife skills, and kitchen equipment operation.

Mentorship programs are available in which one has the opportunity to work directly under a chef. Industry certifications are offered as well. Though not necessary, certifications provide professional designations, a potential increase in opportunities and salary, and of course, training in specific areas.

Chef Leah Schuler started her culinary career as the owner of a catering business. In a 2018 blog post on *We Are Chefs*, Schuler shares why she decided to get certified as a Personal Certified Executive Chef: "I finally got to a point where I was wanting more for my career and didn't want to be defined as just a caterer. I was always interested in Health and Nutrition for my entire adult life, so also wanted to expand on that aspect."

Regardless of one's culinary educational path, it is important for prospective chefs to research license requirements. Some states require an occupational license if a chef wishes to work there.

Skills and Personality

The best chefs are highly creative in crafting menus and creating recipes. They need excellent presentation skills as well as a great sense of taste and smell—not just to produce mouthwatering food but also to check for the quality and freshness of ingredients.

Physically, chefs need good stamina. They work extremely long hours, primarily on their feet. Good eye-hand coordination and manual dexterity are important too, for doing things like slicing, dicing, and ricing. Chefs' most important tools are their knives. High-quality knives are essential. Other much-used tools include graters, whisks, spatulas, pepper grinders, meat grinders, and meat slicers.

Another key skill is being detail oriented. Chefs must juggle many details in order to create recipes, order sufficient ingredients, schedule adequate time for food preparation, and price the menu.

Excellent communication skills are crucial as well for dealing with everyone from suppliers to staff, owners, and customers. People skills, leadership abilities, and expertise in time management will help in overseeing the preparation and serving of food and the accuracy and timeliness of filling a customer's order. And chefs who want to run their own restaurant need to have business skills.

On the Job

Employers

According to the Bureau of Labor Statistics (BLS), there were close to 147,000 chef jobs in 2016. More than half of these jobs were in restaurants or hotels. Other employers of chefs are casinos, cafeterias, resorts, cruise lines, retirement homes, country clubs, and convention centers. Personal and private chefs may work for families, seniors, athletes, and people with specific nutritional needs or in the entertainment business.

Working Conditions

Whether working for someone else or themselves, chefs work in a stressful, fast-paced environment. Kitchens are known for sharp knives, hot ovens, and slippery floors, giving chefs the distinction of having one of the highest rates of injuries and illnesses of all occupations.

Most chefs work long hours, especially during holidays. They often work double and split shifts. This can take a toll on personal relationships. In an interview on the BLS website, Kimberly Brock Brown, a chef in Mount Pleasant, South Carolina, describes some of the demands of the job: "What surprises me still is the amount of time and effort it takes to prepare food. This career requires stamina. The hours are very demanding, and you get tired standing up all day." This is one reason Brown went from working in a hotel kitchen to being a caterer: "I always had an entrepreneurial spirit. After I had my first child, I realized that I wanted to spend more time with my family and still work with food."

Earnings

The median wage for chefs was $45,950 per year as of May 2017, according to the BLS. That means the lowest-paid 10 percent earned less than $25,020, and the highest-paid 10 percent earned more than $78,570. Chefs on the higher end of that pay scale most often worked for prestigious restaurants, hotels, or casinos, especially in major cities or at exclusive resorts.

Opportunities for Advancement

The most talented and creative chefs have the most opportunities for advancement. Having completed a culinary school program combined with solid kitchen experience may also be looked upon favorably by a prospective employer. Those with certifications also have an advantage in this high-turnover, competitive industry. Many chefs leave for better opportunities or to open their own restaurants. That allows others in the kitchen the chance to move up the line. An online career video on the CareerOneStop website, sponsored by the US Department of Labor, explains:

"Advancing in this field may depend as much on limiting food costs and supervising less-skilled workers as it does on creating a memorable menu. To keep things running smoothly in a hot, noisy kitchen, chefs need to be expert multitaskers. The work is fast paced, and a missed detail can result in time lost and wasted food, not to mention an unhappy customer."

What Is the Future Outlook for Chefs?

According to the BLS, chef jobs are expected to grow 10 percent through 2026. That is faster-than-average growth. The increased demand for skilled chefs is being driven by consumers who are looking for higher-quality food experiences and healthier dishes, whether dining out, attending an event, or purchasing ready-made food from a grocery store. There has also been an increase in high-profile chef jobs in the entertainment industry. Many chefs have become household names with their own TV shows.

However, opportunities for women are fewer than for men. Melissa Kravitz explains in a 2018 article in *USA Today*, "Recent data from the U.S. Bureau of Labor Statistics shows that only 19.7% of restaurant kitchens are run by women—a harrowing statistic when 47% of America's workforce is female, and 51% of students enrolled at the Culinary Institute of America are female."

Find Out More

American Culinary Federation (ACF)
180 Center Place Way
St. Augustine, FL 32095
website: www.acfchefs.org

Founded in 1929, the ACF is the largest national professional chefs and cooks association. With more than seventeen thousand members across two hundred chapters, the ACF promotes the culinary profession by being a resource for culinary careers, programs, schools, apprenticeships, scholarships, and certifications.

American Personal & Private Chef Institute (APPCI)
4572 Delaware St.
San Diego, CA 92116
website: www.personalchef.com

An online portal to the private chef industry, the APPCI provides the necessary tools and training to run a personal chef business, including home-study programs.

CareerOneStop
website: www.careeronestop.org

CareerOneStop is a one-stop website sponsored by the US Department of Labor. This informative site features training information, industry resources such as videos, and a career and skill assessment to see whether a person is a good fit for a particular career path. It also has links to state requirements.

United States Chef Association (USCA)
website: www.uschefassoc.com

The USCA is a professional association for chefs that includes training, a job placement service, a chef chat line, and online certifications for sous chefs, executive chefs, and master chefs.

US Personal Chef Association (USPCA)
PO Box 56
Gotha, FL 34734
website: www.uspca.com

Founded in 1992, the USPCA is the largest professional association for private and personal chefs. The USPCA provides certification and food safety training for its members in the United States and beyond.

Hairstylist

What Does a Hairstylist Do?

Hairstylists wash, cut, and style hair—and so much more. Hairstyling is a creative, socially energizing, independent career in which every day offers the possibility of making a difference in someone's life.

Hairstylists are people persons. A good part of their day is spent engaging with clients. A typical appointment usually entails a consultation about the client's hair history and perhaps diagnosing any scalp or hair issues. The stylist then makes style suggestions based the client's desires, hair trends, and the stylist's determination on what would look best.

The stylist washes the client's hair, sometimes giving a revitalizing scalp massage (larger salons have dedicated shampooers), followed by a conditioning treatment. Next the hair is cut and styled. The style might include the hair being colored or highlighted, permed or straightened, or having extensions added or removed. The stylist also shows the client how to maintain the hair's style and recommends hair products or other salon services.

At a Glance

Hairstylist

Minimum Educational Requirements
High school diploma or equivalency

Personal Qualities
Friendly, creative, good eye-hand coordination, manual dexterity, people skills

Licensing
State licensing

Working Conditions
Indoors, full-time, including nights and weekends, on feet most of time

Salary Range
About $18,000 to $50,000 or more

Number of Jobs
More than 617,000 as of 2016*

Future Job Outlook
Growth of 13 percent through 2026

* Includes hairdressers, hairstylists, and cosmetologists

Most hairstylists spend as much time getting to know their clients as they do cutting and styling hair. The job requires someone who can do both at the same time.

Stylists have other duties, including scheduling appointments, sanitizing and sterilizing tools, and keeping their workstation clean and organized. A stylist's basic tools include scissors, various types of combs and brushes, a hair dryer and diffuser, both flat and curling irons, clips, and pins—and all of these must be kept clean and sanitary.

Stylists who own their own salons must also do business tasks like managing, scheduling, and training staff; maintaining employee and client records; ordering supplies and products; tracking inventory; marketing the salon; and possibly performing basic bookkeeping tasks. A hairstylist must also keep up with the latest hair trends and new products on the market.

But the most important thing a hairstylist does is make people happy. A big part of the job is ensuring that clients feel good about their services, especially if the hairstylist wants to build a loyal clientele. In *U.S. News & World Report*'s "Best Jobs Rankings" for 2018, hairstylist Scott J. Buchanan says: "There's so much more to what we do than cutting hair. . . . We also get to change people's lives and make them feel good about themselves."

Buchanan, who owns Scott J. Salons & Spas in New York City, further explains on his website, ScottJ:

> As a high-school dropout, owning one hair salon—let alone multiple salons—was a career path I never dreamed of pursuing. . . .
>
> It was one day at a time, one guest at a time. I focused on giving a great experience to everyone in my chair. I will always remember the first time a client cried when I told her she was beautiful. I told her I wanted to emphasize her beautiful cheekbones and eyes, and then I saw tears coming down her face. Making people feel good about themselves is what I love, and has been driving my passion since day one.

How Do You Become a Hairstylist?

Education

Some high schools offer cosmetology courses, which would be a great start for anyone considering a career as a hairstylist. A high school diploma (or equivalency) is not always required to be a stylist. However, every state requires hairstylists to complete a program at a state-licensed cosmetology school, and a diploma will most likely be required for that.

There are very few dedicated hairstylist schools. Most are part of a larger cosmetology program that also includes classes on skin care, makeup, and nails. Cosmetology programs are available at community colleges as well as beauty or cosmetology schools. These programs combine traditional classroom learning with hands-on practice on mannequins and hair models.

In addition to various hairstyling-related courses, students will also take classes in customer service, color theory, hair pathology, hair product analysis, and sanitation and sterilization practices. Stylists who plan to open their own salon may also take business, sales, and marketing courses.

Most certificate and diploma programs take from nine to twelve months to complete. An associate's degree is usually two years and includes a number of non-beauty courses as well. The length of the program is determined by the number of hours required by the state licensing board, so it is important to check state requirements when choosing a program. Bachelor's degree programs are available as well, but they focus on business in addition to hairstyling.

The cost for programs ranges from $6,000 to as much as $20,000, depending on the length of the program as well as state residency laws. Some programs require stylists to pay for their own tools, but some include the tools with tuition. Programs in larger cities, such as New York City, usually cost more. And stylists who wish to specialize in the entertainment industry may need further training. But all hairstylists are lifelong learners and must keep up-to-date on the latest hairstyles and products.

Licensing

All states require hairstylists to be licensed. Licensees must be at least sixteen years old and graduates of a state-approved cosmetology program. Licensing requires an exam, which usually includes both a written test and a practical-skills test.

Few states offer licenses just for hairstyling. Most offer cosmetology licenses. Some states require cosmetologists to update their education and renew their license at set intervals. And some state boards will allow stylists to get a license in another state without retesting.

Skills and Personality

Hairstylists have a certain set of skills. The best hairstylists are creative and have a great sense of style. They also need to be friendly and sociable. Good communication skills—especially listening skills—are important for successful client relationships.

Certain physical skills are required as well. Manual and finger dexterity is a requisite for this career. Physical stamina is required as well because hairstylists are constantly on their feet.

Stylists need to be organized. They must keep a clean workstation for health and safety reasons. They also need good time-management skills because they are often juggling clients and timed treatments.

And finally, stylists need a good knowledge of sales and marketing. Stylists, especially self-employed stylists, need to promote themselves, their products, and their businesses.

On the Job

Employers

The Bureau of Labor Statistics (BLS) groups hairstylists, hairdressers, and cosmetologists into one occupational group. In 2016 they held more than 617,000 jobs.

According to the BLS, approximately 52 percent of this group work in the personal care industry at salons, spas, hotels, and resorts. Many others—43 percent, in fact—are self-employed. Some work out of their homes, some lease booth space from salons, and some freelance on-site at weddings or on location for film, magazine, photography, or TV productions. And some of these professionals work privately for celebrities and models.

Some hairstylists work in other industries. These include jobs as beauty school teachers, beauty magazine contributors (or editors), and sales representatives for beauty product companies.

Working Conditions

Conditions can be physically demanding for hairstylists. Stylists work both part-time and full-time—on their feet—and their busiest times are evenings and weekends. And stylists who work in the entertainment business should be prepared to work even longer hours. However, self-employed stylists can set their own schedules.

Melissa Mayntz interviewed celebrity hairstylist Billy Lowe for the *LoveToKnow* blog. Lowe, located in Beverly Hills, California, has worked as Ellen DeGeneres's personal stylist. He says, "It takes hours upon hours upon hours to do hair for the camera.

Whenever you're preparing hair to be camera-ready, every scene has a consistency check to make sure everything is accurate. The hair has to be consistent for all camera angles, and even a simple magazine shoot can take 1–2 hours of preparation. You're also there all day touching up between scenes."

Stylists are also exposed to toxic chemicals. Hair-processing chemicals, for example, may cause skin irritation, so stylists need to take safety precautions and wear protective clothing.

Job stress is an issue for most hairstylists. Stress is high if a client is not happy with the final results. But the flip side is that when a client is satisfied, it is very rewarding. Buchanan, who once did makeovers for audience members on *The Oprah Winfrey Show*, speaks to this on the *U.S. News & World Report* website: "When I say to someone, 'Let's enhance the shape of your face with this type of haircut,' and then to watch their face light up and see how grateful they are when they see the outcome—I still get goose bumps."

Earnings

The BLS states that the median annual salary for hairdressers, hairstylists, and cosmetologists was about $25,000 in 2017. The lowest-paid 10 percent earned about $18,000, and the highest-paid 10 percent earned more than $50,000.

A stylist's salary is dependent on experience and location. Larger cities usually mean larger salaries. Earnings are also enhanced by client tips and product commissions. And for self-employed individuals, how they market their services and build their clientele directly affects their wages.

Opportunities for Advancement

The beauty industry is very competitive. Some cosmetology students work in salons as shampooers while getting their education. Knowing how a salon works can give them both an advantage and a foot in the door once they are licensed.

The more experience a stylist has, the more opportunities exist for advancement to management positions and therefore better pay. Staying on top of the latest hair trends helps, as well as having training or experience in all cosmetology services like makeup, skin, and nails. Stylists can also advance by becoming self-employed. High-demand stylists with a steady and loyal clientele often open their own shops.

Specializing as a private stylist can also advance a stylist's career. These stylists need to create a portfolio of their best work and promote it online via their own websites or social media accounts. Private stylists often find clients by volunteering on movie sets or at photo shoots or by obtaining an agent.

Buchanan suggests that students who want to advance in this industry align themselves with a good beauty school. He recommends that they work in a salon for at least a year and work on people skills. "That's when you get to hone your craft," Buchanan says in *U.S. News & World Report*. "You have to have an outgoing personality and be ready to serve the customer."

What Is the Future Outlook for Hairstylists?

Hairstyling is a growth industry. According to the BLS, there is expected to be a 13 percent increase in hairstylists, hairdressers, and cosmetologists through 2026. This will equal roughly eighty thousand new jobs.

Driving this growth (which is faster than average for all occupations) are many factors, including an increasing population. There is also a need to replace stylists who are retiring or leaving the industry. Add to that a steady increase in the demand for advanced hair treatments like coloring and straightening—something that is expected to continue—and it is easy to see why this is a growing industry.

Find Out More

American Association of Cosmetology Schools (AACS)
9927 E. Bell Rd., Suite 110
Scottsdale, AZ 85260
website: http://beautyschools.org

The AACS, an organization of national, privately owned cosmetology schools, was founded in 1924. Its website features a career section, where students interested in a career as a hairstylist can find information on related schools, webinars, online training, licensing and accreditation requirements (by state), grants, and scholarships.

Beauty Schools Directory
website: www.beautyschoolsdirectory.com

The directory, which has over five hundred schools listed, can assist students interested in a hairstylist career in finding schools, state board requirements, scholarships, financial aid, accreditation, licensing information, and jobs.

CareerOneStop
website: www.careeronestop.org

CareerOneStop is a one-stop website sponsored by the US Department of Labor. This informative site features training information, industry resources such as videos, and state licensing requirements. There is also a career and ability skill assessment to see whether a person is a good fit for a particular career path.

Professional Beauty Association (PBA)
website: www.probeauty.org

The PBA is the largest association of salon professionals. Its website provides live educational events, resources, webinars, online on-demand training, and scholarship information for cosmetology students.

Interview with a Hairstylist

Stephanie Ainsworth Kondzela is a hairstylist with close to three decades' experience in the business. She left a career as a flight attendant in her early twenties to become a hairstylist. Kondzela has worked in a salon and been self-employed. Over the course of her career, she has worked for only a handful of salons, which she acknowledges is low for this industry. She currently works for a hair salon in San Diego, California, and answered questions by e-mail and phone.

Q: Why did you become a hairstylist?
A: I fell into hair because I had a friend who was a hair dresser. I'd been working as a flight attendant based in New York and quit after the 1988 terrorist bombing of Pam Am Flight 103 over Lockerbie, Scotland. It was too close for comfort. I got scared. I had six roommates at the time. Five were flight attendants and one a hairstylist. It sounded like it would be fun. I didn't have a lot of alternatives because I hadn't finished community college and needed something to do, so I took a ten-month program.

Q: Can you describe your typical workday?
A: Every day is different. Some days are quick cuts, many in a row. Sometimes it's a mixture of haircuts and color appointments. And sometimes it's long and arduous, like five to seven hours of just color service.

Q: What do you like most about your job?
A: I love the people, relationships, and satisfaction of a completed job well done. I also like the flexibility of my schedule.

Q: What do you like least about your job?
A: I don't love the organization part of my work: making and confirming appointments; managing my color/supplies; and banking and managing money. I also dislike having to deal with unhappy or depressed people sometimes.

Q: What's the worst part about dealing with clients?
A: I had to learn to set boundaries. When you're first starting out, you're at the beck-and-call of your clients. You want to make money and you also want to please everyone, so you make exceptions to your schedule. Otherwise they just go to someone else. At first it gives you a feeling of importance, but you soon get burned out working long hours and giving up your own time to fit someone else's. I had to learn to set my schedule and keep it. The clients now have to fit my schedule, and if not, I have to be okay if they go elsewhere.

Q: Do you sometimes feel like a therapist to your clients?
A: All the time! They tell you everything—what's going on with their children; their bodies. It's a relationship and it's like we're friends. Clients will tell you if they're feeling good, if they love their hair that day, or if they're sad or unhappy. I love people. And for many years I tried to help them, but now I let them be responsible for their own feelings. It's just part of the job.

Q: How do you deal with clients who are unhappy with their hair?
A: When I was first starting out, people often came in saying they wanted their hair to look like Jennifer Aniston's, for example. I'd do my best, but sometimes it wasn't what they wanted. They weren't precise enough in what they said they wanted, or maybe we had different ideas of what that looked like because Aniston wore her hair different ways at different times. But now, after this many years in the business, I've learned it's easy to give people what they want if I'm a good communicator. If I'm very clear, it's easy to have happy and satisfied clients. For example, I might explain how the hairstyle they want is going to take a lot of main-

tenance and I know they don't like to spend time on their hair. It's easier now because I've built relationships. So if my client is having a bad day, all I can do is my best. I don't feel responsible anymore.

Q: What personal qualities do you find most valuable for this type of work?
A: The personal qualities that come in handy for me are being compassionate and caring; being a good listener; having a good memory; being playful, artistic and fun; and seeing the good qualities and inner beauty in all people and then sharing with them. Time management is also important.

Q: What is the best way to prepare for this type of job?
A: Education, practice and then continued education is the way to prepare and be successful.

Q: What other advice do you have for students who might be interested in this career?
A: Get educated, stay educated and practice. It's a wonderful career with many perks. Set your boundaries and have fun!

Other Jobs in the Skilled Trades

Aircraft & avionic equipment mechanic
Aircraft assembler
Bicycle repairer
Boilermaker
Bricklayer
Carpenter
Cement mason
Commercial diver
Construction worker
Cosmetologist
Diesel mechanic
Drafter
Drywaller
Electronics technician
Elevator installer and repairer
Exterminator
Farm equipment mechanic
Forklift operator
Glazier
Heating, ventilation, and air-conditioning technician
Industrial machinery repairer
Lineman
Locksmith
Machinist
Manicurist, pedicurist
Millwright
Mortician
Motorcycle mechanic
Painter
Photographer
Refrigeration mechanic and installer
Sheet metal worker
Shipfitter
Shoe repairer
Solderer, brazer
Steelworker
Tile and marble installer
Tool and die maker
Tractor trailer driver
Transit driver

Editor's Note: The US Department of Labor's Bureau of Labor Statistics provides information about hundreds of occupations. The agency's *Occupational Outlook Handbook* describes what these jobs entail, the work environment, education and skill requirements, pay, future outlook, and more. The *Occupational Outlook Handbook* may be accessed online at www.bls.gov/ooh.

Index

Note: Boldface page numbers indicate illustrations.

Adams, Jono, 17, 18, 20
American Association of Cosmetology Schools (AACS), 71–72
American Culinary Federation (ACF), 63
American Personal & Private Chef Institute (APPCI), 64
American Welding Society (AWS), 7, 27, 31–32
American Wind Energy Association (AWEA), 55
apprenticeships, 5, 7. *See also specific careers*
arc welding, 25
Automotive Service Association (ASA), 40
Automotive Service Excellence (ASE) certification, 36–37
automotive technician
  advancement opportunities, 39
  certification, 33, 36–37
  educational requirements, 33, 35–36
  employers of, 37–38
  future job outlook, 33, 39
  information resources, 40
  number of jobs, 33
  role of, 33–35
  salary/earnings, 33, 38–39
  skills/personal qualities, 33, 37
  working conditions, 33, 38
Automotive Youth Educational Systems (AYES), 40

Beauty Schools Directory (website), 72
Bence, Laurie, 14
"Best Jobs Rankings" (*U.S. News & World Report*)
  on automotive technician, 34, 38
  on electrician, 21
  on hairstylist, 66
  on plumber, 14
  on PV installer, 44
Brock, Kimberly, 62
Buchanan, Scott J., 66–67, 70, 71
Bureau of Labor Statistics, 7, 76
  on automotive technician, 37–38, 39
  on chef, 61, 62, 63
  on electrician, 21–22, 23
  on hairstylist, 69, 70, 71
  on plumber, 12, 13, 14, 15
  on PV installer, 45, 46
  on welder, 29, 30–31
  on wind turbine technician, 52, 54, 55

Career Foundation, 4
CareerOneStop (website), 32, 40, 62–63, 64, 72
Careers in Welding (website), 32
Cartwright, Bethany, 29
Chamber of Commerce, US, 5

chef, **58**
   advancement opportunities, 62–63
   apprenticeships, 60
   certification/licensing, 57, 60
   educational requirements, 57, 59–60
   employers of, 61
   future job outlook, 57, 63
   information resources, 63–64
   number of jobs, 57
   role of, 57–59
   salary/earnings, 57, 62
   skills/personal qualities, 57, 61
   working conditions, 57, 62
Commercial Construction Index (United States Gypsum, US Chamber of Commerce), 5

Department of Labor, US, 32
Ditch the Desk (Ecotech Institute), 42, 51, 52–53, 54, 55

Ecotech Institute, 42, 47, 52, 56
Electrical Training Alliance, 23
electrician
   advancement opportunities, 22
   apprenticeships, 19–20
   certification/licensing, 17, 19–20
   educational requirements, 17, 18
   employers of, 21
   future job outlook, 17, 22–23
   information resources, 23–24
   number of jobs, 17
   role of, 17–18
   salary/earnings, 17, 21–22
   skills/personal qualities, 17, 20
   working conditions, 17, 21
Electrician Careers Guide (website), 7–8, 18, 22, 23
ElectricianSchoolEdu.org (website), 23
Ellyn, Emily, 58–59
ePlumbingCourses (website), 13–14, 15
Explore the Trades, 24

Garber, Allen, 26

hairstylist, **66**
   advancement opportunities, 70–71
   educational requirements, 65, 67–68
   employers of, 69
   future job outlook, 65, 71
   information resources, 71–72
   interview with, 73–75
   licensing, 65, 68
   number of jobs, 65
   role of, 65–67
   salary/earnings, 65, 70
   skills/personal qualities, 65, 68–69
   working conditions, 65, 69–70
Higgins, Jerry, 19, 20
high school diploma, 4
Howard, Don, 29

Independent Electrical Contractors (IEC), 24
Interstate Renewable Energy Council (IREC), 48

Jones, Dave, 10, 15

Kellett, Patrick, 12–13
Kilroy, Jessica, 50
Kondzela, Stephanie Ainsworth, 73–75
Kravitz, Melissa, 63

Larson, Diane, 34
licensing, 5

Mayntz, Melissa, 69–70
mikeroweWORKS Foundation, 26, 32

National Electrical Contractors Association (NECA), 24
National Institute for Automotive Service Excellence (ASE) Education Foundation, 40

Occupational Information Network (O*NET) Online (website), 56
Occupational Outlook Handbook (Bureau of Labor Statistics), 12, 31, 76
Odle, Constance, 44, 45–46
Office of Energy Efficiency & Renewable Energy (EERE), 42, 48, 56

Pick My Solar (blog), 47
pipefitter, 13
plumber, **11**
  advancement opportunities, 14
  apprenticeships, 10–12
  certification/licensing, 9, 10–12
  educational requirements, 9, 10
  employers of, 13
  future job outlook, 9, 14–15
  information resources, 15–16
  number of jobs, 9
  role of, 9–10
  salary/earnings, 9, 14
  skills/personal qualities, 9, 12–13
  working conditions, 9, 13–14
Plumbing & Mechanical (online magazine), 14

Plumbing Contractors of America (PCA), 15
Plumbing-Heating-Cooling Contractors Association (PHCC), 16
PlumbingWEB.com (website), 16
Professional Beauty Association (PBA), 72
PV installer. *See* solar photovoltaic installer

Roamer, Paul, 54
Roof Integrated Solar Energy (Rise) Inc., 48
Rowe, Mike, 26

Schuler, Leah, 60
Shriver, Scott, 26
skilled trades, 4
  educational requirements/pay for occupations in, 5
  other jobs in, 76
  women in, 7–8
Solar Energy International (SEI), 48
solar photovoltaic (PV) installer, **43**
  advancement opportunities, 46–47
  apprenticeships/certification, 41, 44
  educational requirements, 41, 42–44
  employers of, 45
  future job outlook, 41, 46–47
  information resources, 47–48
  number of jobs, 41
  role of, 41–42
  salary/earnings, 41, 46
  skills/personal qualities, 41, 44
  working conditions, 41, 45–46
steamfitter, 13

That's Amazing (TV program), 50
ToughNickel (website), 17
Trump, Donald, 7

underwater welding, 25–26
United Association of Journeymen and Apprentices of the Plumbing and Pipe Fitting Industry of the United States, Canada (UA), 16
United Association—Union of Plumbers, Fitters, Welders and Service Techs, 7
United States Chef Association (USCA), 64
United States Gypsum, 5
USA Today (newspaper), 63
U.S. News & World Report (magazine), 12–13, 53, 70, 71
US Personal Chef Association (USPCA), 64

Van Slyke, Auston, 52, 53

welder, **28**
   advancement opportunities, 30
   apprenticeships, 27–28
   certification/licensing, 25, 27–28
   educational requirements, 25, 27
   employers of, 29
   future job outlook, 25, 30–31
   information resources, 31–32
   number of jobs, 25
   role of, 25–26
   salary/earnings, 25, 30
   skills/personal qualities, 25, 28–29
   working conditions, 25, 29–30
wind turbine technician
   advancement opportunities, 54
   certification/training, 49, 51–52
   educational requirements, 49, 51
   employers of, 52–53
   future job outlook, 49, 55
   information resources, 55–56
   number of jobs, 49
   role of, 49–50
   salary/earnings, 49, 54
   skills/personal qualities, 49, 52
   working conditions, 49, 53–54
WindTurbineTechnicians.net, 56
women
   as chefs, 63
   as electricians, 23
   in plumbing, 14
   in skilled trades, 7–8
   in welding, 31
Wright, Veronica, 47